Bear Hunt

Anthony Browne

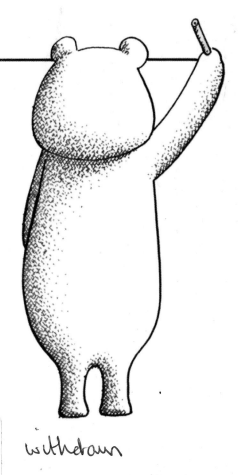

PUFFIN

One day Bear went for a walk.

Two hunters were hunting.

They saw Bear.

Look out! Look out, Bear!

Quickly Bear began to draw.

Well done, Bear!

But there was another hunter.

Run, Bear, run!

Out came Bear's pencil.

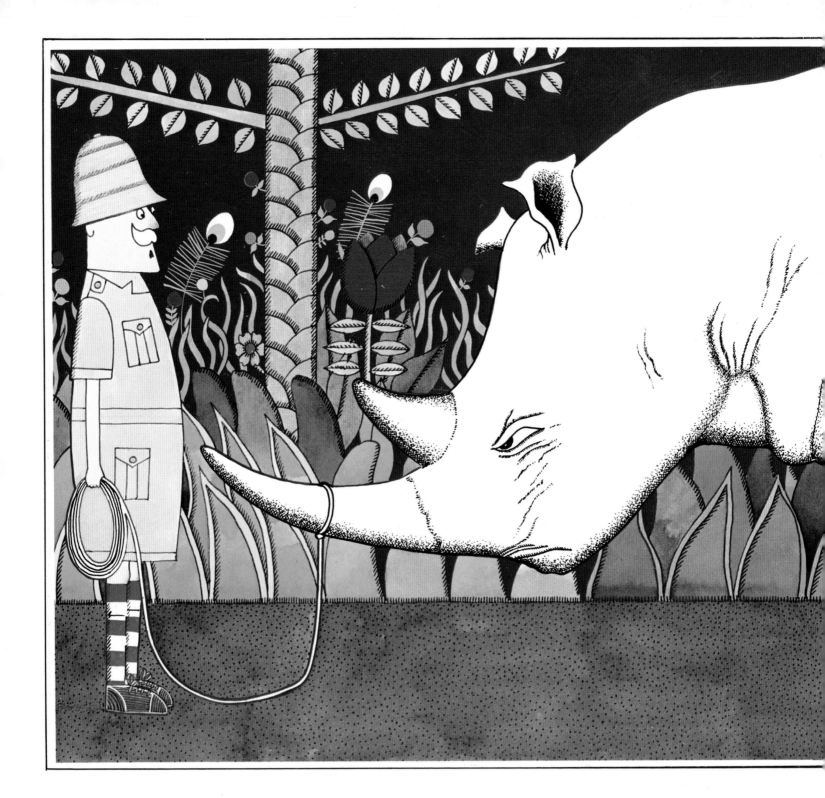

And Bear walked on.

Stop! The hunter's back . . .

Swiftly Bear got to work.

Look up, Bear!

Bear is caught.

But Bear still had his pencil . . .

Clever Bear!

HELP – !

Do something, Bear!

So Bear escaped . . .

. . . and the hunters were left far, far behind.